Clara
the Cookie Fairy

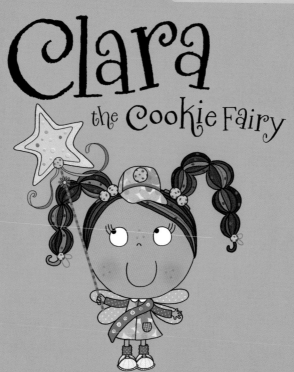

Tim Bugbird · Lara Ede

make
believe
ideas

Once there were three Fairy Scouts — Clara, Kat and Jan,
who lived upon a mountain in a fairy camper van.

COOKI

They sold special cookies – a Fairy-Scout tradition –
buy the things they needed for their camping expeditions!

Clara's wand made cookies,
tasty, crisp and sweet,

nd Kat's made **pretty** boxes
o keep them nice and **neat**.

Last of all, Jan's wand made a special fairy **bow**.
n every cookie **baked** and **boxed**, the friends were good to go!

Then, one **summer's** evening, they were driving out to dine
when Clara's eye was caught by a **giant** roadside sign.

COOKIES

The sign read:

MIGHTY
MEGA-WANDS

make cookies with chocolate chips!

Clara said, "I want one now! I can't let this chance slip!"

Clara picked the biggest wand and stood in line to pay.
Her old one looked too boring
so she threw
it right away!

Pay here

Rubbish

But Clara **wasn't** careful and her wand was a little **brittle**

She **whooshed**

and **swooshed** it way too much

The fairies tried to fix the wand
with **string** and **tape** and **glue**.
But not one thing would make it **work**.
Now what could they do?

Kat said, "Only **one** thing will put us back on track –
we must find the **fairy dustcart**
and get your old wand **back!**"

The fairies drove across the land,

searching high and low,

'til Jan saw a scrapyard

in a meadow

down

below.

Scrap

Unwanted wands were everywhere –
the place was overrun!
Lots looked just like Clara's,
so they tried them one by one.

The **friends** spent many hours waving wands **around**. But **not one** of them made cookies. Clara's wand could not be **found!**

The fairies were getting **worried**.

Things weren't going well.

How would they fund their **camping trip** if they had no **cookies** to sell?

Then Clara said, "**Stop!** Look down!"
And **suddenly** it was clear.
What the wands **had** been making
was fairy **camping gear!**

There were
pots and pans,
forks and spoons,
kettles and cans
and guitars to play tunes!

There were balls and bats,
three fairy bikes,
bright summer hats
and boots for long hikes!

"These **wands** should be **used**,

not thrown away,"

said Clara with a frown.

"But if we put our heads together,

we can turn this **right around**!"

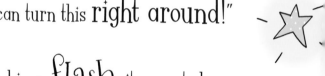

And in a **flash** it came to her,

a **new** Fairy-Scouting venture.

They'd move to the **meadow**

and transform the yard

into a **Swap and Recycling Centre!**

Fairies came from far and wide
with their wands, unwanted or broken,
to swap or make into something new.
The centre was always open!